Yahweh Publication Presents

Unleashed Penning

Mrs. Malin Jenifer Raja

Yahweh Publication

Tamilnadu, India

yahweh_publication

Yahweh Publication

yahwehpublication@gmail.com

9363734705

Your words, our passion!

Yahweh Publication proudly presents,

Unleashed Penning (Vol 1).

ISBN: 978-81-991357-4-1.

First edition: September 2025.

Compiled by: Mrs. Malin Jenifer Raja.

Cover design: Yahweh Publication.

Book formatting: Yahweh Publication.

Disclaimer

This book, Unleashed Penning, is a work of fiction. All names, characters and incidents portrayed in this book are either a product of the author's imagination or are used factiously. Any resemblance to actual persons, living or dead, or actual events is purely coincidental.

Every effort has been made to ensure the accuracy and integrity of the material after obtaining the writer's consent. However, the authors and Yahweh Publication declaim any liability for any loss, damage or disruption caused by errors of omissions, whether resulting from negligence, accident or any other cause. Yahweh Publication endeavors to present error-free content, but we do not assume responsibility for any inadvertent mistakes. In cases of plagiarism, sole responsibility lies with the co-authors; the publisher disclaims liability.

This book is a product of Yahweh Publication's dedicated efforts. Yahweh Publication and compilers bear no responsibility for any plagiarized co tent. Only co-authors are accountable in the event of plagiarism. It is important to note that this book does not intend to disrespect any community, caste, religion, creed, nationality or gender.

- R. Malin Jenifer.
- Founder & CEO.

Acknowledgement

First & foremost, thanks to the Almighty for the blessings & strength to complete this project.

To the poets, writers & contributors who shared their words, emotions & experiences with me, I offer my deepest gratitude. Your voices, perspectives, & creativity have enriched this anthology, making it a testament to the power of language & human connection.

To those who have faced challenges, overcome struggles, & found solace in words, this anthology is a celebration of your resilience & spirit.

May these poems inspire, comfort, & resonate with readers, reminding them that they are not alone in their journeys.

- R. Malin Jenifer.
- Compiler.

About the book

Step into the kaleidoscope of human experience, where stories, emotions, & moments burst forth in vibrant colors. 'Unleashed Penning' is a masterful curation of these fragments, woven together by a diverse chorus of voices, styles, & perspectives. United by the threads of various themes, this anthology is a testament to the boundless creativity and depth of the human spirit. Within these pages, you'll discover tales that ignite, provoke, & soothe – a symphony of words that will resonate long after the final sentence. Join us on a journey that traverses the highs & lows, the triumphs & struggles, & and the moments that make us who we are. Let the words transport you, challenge you, & connect you to the very essence of humanity. Dive in & let the stories unfold!

Read this book and enjoy. Thank you!

FOUNDER AND CEO OF YAHWEH PUBLICATION

Mrs. R. Malin Jenifer

Mrs. R. Malin Jenifer, daughter of Mr. M. Raja & Mrs. R. Beula and wife of Mr. Martin Manoah. She is a mother of two kids. And, she is an optimistic and energetic person with a big dream from a small town in Ooty. She is a post graduate in Biochemistry and she holds a Diploma in Bio-informatics. Though she is a life science graduate, her interest towards art and literature made her a writer. She has worked as an Online tutor and an assistant professor at different organizations. She is the person who is basically an extrovert and selectively an introvert. She strongly believes in the destination and karma. And, her hope relies on the patience and hard-work. As a follower of Christ, she has a strong belief in a Bible verse *(Phil 4:13)* that says, *'I can do all the things through Christ which strengtheneth me'* and she completely trusts the word and plan of God. She believes that her day starts with the blessings of Christ and ends at his feet. She is the person who seeks for the recognition for her work and she believes that this publication is the first step of it. And currently, she is playing roles like writer, compiler and project head under different publications.

She can be contacted through her mail yahwehpublication@gmail.com and her Instagram handle: yahweh_publication.

Theme: The hidden truth

Writers:

- Malin Jenifer Raja.
- Dr. Richa Biswal.
- Divya D Nayak.
- Blessy Rani Jenefer S.
- Tr Mrs Sunita Martins.
- Hershey.
- Pavithra.
- Dr. Rutam Biswal.

Untouched by words

Does every feeling need to be expressed in words?

Not every bird that wears wings flies high,

Still the purpose remains, exchanged.

Not every artwork needs dye,

Still its beauty endures, unchanged.

Some feelings remain unspoken,

Delicate buds untouched by words.

It doesn't always have to be broken,

Can also be happy chords.

The essence of unverbalized stays intact

Even if it is unveiled in language.

Here, our authors have poured their heart out

Get ready to taste the different thoughts.

Welcome to join the warm stage!

- *Malin Jenifer R.*

The Hidden Truth

Beneath the smile, beneath the grace,

Lies a truth time can't erase.

Behind each word so sweetly said,

A tale untold, a tear unshed.

In mirror's glass we show a face,

But not the storms we must embrace.

The world sees light, but not the flame,

That burns in silence, without name.

A thousand masks we wear with ease,

To soothe the world, ourselves to please.

Yet deep within, a voice confined,

Still seeks the courage to unwind.

A truth we hide with woven care,

Like thread unseen in fabric fair.

For fear, or love, or simple peace -

We guard it so, we grant no lease.

But hidden truth, though wrapped in shade,

Will find a crack in walls we've made.

A whisper first, then roaring tide,

It breaks the lock where shadows hide.

And when it stands in naked light,

It does not scream; it does not fight.

It simply is - no need to prove,

And frees the soul it could not move.

- *Dr. Richa Biswal.*

Hidden Truth

Born a kitty with no eyes

Tried to grew up them

Some days, Some month

Kitties were given to someone

Unknown Unknown

Truth was hide, lie to him

Need to be quiet

Hidden Truth, Hidden Trust

Hide cry, Lost my kitty

Pray to God, Trust inner.

- *Divya D Nayak.*

Echoes of the Unspoken

In silent rooms where secrets sleep,
Where shadows stretch and memories creep,
A truth lies buried, soft and deep
Too bold to speak, too shy to weep.
It wears no crown, it claims no fame,
It hides behind a borrowed name.
A fleeting thought, a subtle sign,
A thread that slips through woven time.
It hums beneath the noise of day,
In things we throw, in words we say.
It flickers in a lover's sigh,
Then vanishes as moments fly.
It waits in dreams we dare not name,
In echoes lost to love and shame.
A whisper caught in time's embrace,
A tear that leaves no outward trace.
And when the night grows still and wide,

It walks beside us, not to hide.

For truth, though veiled in quiet hue,

Will find the hearts that seek what's true.

Not every truth is meant to rise,

Some bloom beneath indifferent skies.

They live in silence, not in proof,

The quiet grace of hidden truth.

\- *Blessy Rani Jenefer S.*

Hidden Truth

There is some hidden truth in what I say and at times it is
difficult to disclose it to anyone for that matter.

The hidden truth could be something that hurt us and we
keep it hidden for years on end as these things to us do
matter.

It's the bitter truth that remained with you and your heart
cried every time you remembered it for no fault of yours.

There is some hidden truth which at times you want to
disclose for that is the truth that has made you upset,
stressed and very sad.

When the hidden truth comes to your mind that's when
you got back into your shell and then you yell and go
mad.

The hidden truth will no longer be hidden anymore for
the time has come to be open to someone and that is at
some point in your life.

Show the world my dearest friends that we human
beings need a shoulder to lean on and to open up when
we feel let down in our lives.

- *Tr Mrs Sunita Martins.*

The Things I Don't Post

I smile like I mean it, click, then scroll
But no one knows when I start to fold.
My coffee's cold, my heart's on mute,
I'm dressed in strength but stripped of truth.
I say, "I'm fine," like it's gospel word,
But it echoes hollow, barely heard.
They see my wins, my curated frame,
Not the nights I whisper Jesus' name.
They don't see how my stomach churns,
When I crave the food but the acid burns.
They don't see me clean the floor,
While my thoughts spiral more and more.
OCD's a quiet, brutal guest,
It scrubs my peace, denies me rest.
I hide my tremble in typed replies,
But grief still haunts behind my eyes.

They praise the poise, the put-together,

Not the girl braving stormy weather.

Not the daughter praying her dad stays near

Folding hope into every tear.

I was number one - they clap for that,

But they didn't see the weight, the spat

Between who I am and who they think,

Between the spotlight and the brink.

I've turned down deals, walked out of rooms,

Said no to trends, ignored the zooms.

Cause I don't want fame, I want free.

A soul that roars, not just agrees.

I'm not your "nice girl," "soft and sweet,"

I'm thorns and healing, raw and beat.

I'm every verse in Hebrews cried,

Every part of me that nearly died.

Yet here I stand, all cracked and bold,

Not every scar needs to be told.

But some nights. yeah—I write them down,

To remind myself I didn't drown.

So, if you feel too much, too deep,

If silence haunts you when you sleep

You're not alone. You never were.

The fight inside is not a blur.

We wear our masks, but here's the key:

The rawest hearts still choose to be.

To show up tired, to show up real

That, my friend, is how we heal.

- *Hershey.*

Hidden Truth

The truth was hidden,

And that's okay.

But the reason behind it,

Broke my heart;

You weren’t too busy to hide the truth,

You were simply not ready to share it with me.

And you never want to be ready,

And that hurts me deeply.

- *Pavithra.*

Whispers in the Library's Breath

In the hush where the lamplight falls,
Through the endless, towering walls,
Books stand guard like patient kings,
Holding the weight of a thousand things.
The air is warm with a paper scent,
Of ink long dry, of years well spent,
Yet more than lessons, dates, or lore,
These halls conceal an unseen store.
Each volume, bound in velvet hue,
Is dressed in titles proud and true,
But in its heart, beyond the show,
It hides the things we'll never know.
The history text may praise the crown,
But not the hands that pulled it down,
It marks the years, the wars, the reigns,
Yet skips the blood on silent chains.

The poet's work may hum in rhyme,
Yet leave unsaid a darker time,
The math that solves the longest sum,
Won't speak of nights when hope felt numb.
The student bends with weary eyes,
Through fading dusk and midnight skies,
He learns the facts, the rules, the frame,
Yet wonders if he plays a game.
For truth is sly, it does not shout,
It hides in corners, slips about,
It's in the footnotes none will read,
It's in the silence where thoughts bleed.

A scientist may chart the star,
And tell you just how far they are,
But not the dreams that made him try,
Nor fears that asked the question "why?"
The teacher stands before the class,
With wisdom's torch held high to pass,

Yet some truths live too deep to share,
Too raw, too strange, too hard to bear.
In libraries, the shadows grow,
Between the shelves where few will go,
The dust that dances in the light,
Knows every secret hid from sight.
For books are mirrors, veiled in gold,
They guard the truths they can't be told,
You read the tale, but not the ache,
You see the bridge, but not the break.
So read the words, but read between,
The gloss, the shine, the printed sheen,
For somewhere past the scholar's view,
The hidden truth still waits for you.

And when the final page is turned,
When every lesson's weight is learned,
You'll find that knowledge, deep and wide,
Still leaves a door unlatched inside -

A place where whispers weave their thread,

Of all the things that went unsaid,

Were hidden truths, in quiet breath,

Outlive the bounds of time and death.

- *Dr. Rutam Biswal.*

Theme: Grandma's kitchen.

Writers:

- Malin Jenifer Raja.
- Tr Mrs Sunita Martins.
- Subholaxmi Ganguly.
- Blessy Rani Jenefer S.
- Priyadharshini K.
- Dr. Richa Biswal.
- Sakshi Kshipra Singh.
- Divya D Nayak.
- Dr. Rutam Biswal.

Her kitchen! Her own recipes!

When she cooks, senses come alive,
A symphony of flavors, aroma thrive.
Flavor's bloom, wonders unfold,
Her kitchen's magic, a treasure to behold.
No hotel's fare can compare,
By her side, hunger fades like air.
Her love simmers in every bite,
Love served with every dish, so sweet.
Grandma's kitchen, a haven of love,
Flavors of childhood, stays above.
Each dish a tale, warmth in each bite,
Unforgettable moments, that forever last.

Dive into the flavors of her kitchen,
Through the words of our authors written.

\- *Malin Jenifer R.*

Grandma's Kitchen.

My grandma's kitchen is a place where everyone wants
to be there time and again for the delicious dishes' that
she prepares with love and care.

My grandma is a great cook, everyone loves to eat the
yummy food prepared by her, using her own unique
recipes and then some will stare.

My grandma's kitchen has become so very famous that
she is often asked to come over, if possible, to cook for
someone out there.

When she lays the table with her tasty and delicious
dishes' there is hunger to attack her food before time
since it is made with so much care

My grandma's kitchen has a place for anyone who wants
to try preparing food under her guidance and advice she
is always ready to share.

My grandma's kitchen is a ritually blessed place so to say
for any new person who enters there finds himself or
herself feeling hungry and their hunger is hard to bear.

So friends I would like to ask you all who are food
lovers to come over and try my grandma's dishes' I
promise you, you will not regret.

My grandma's kitchen is and will always be my greatest memory to have eaten such great food that I will always find hard to get.

- *Tr Mrs Sunita Martins.*

The Best Kitchen- Grandma's Kitchen

Calling us to ask which fish is to be made,

Secretly filling our mouth with chochos of varied shades.

Each chamber waved at us with something very sweet,

Grandma guarded the kitchen door so that we could naughtily eat.

An extra cube of butter was confirmed with grandma inside,

A bowl of sugar was set aside for us to enjoy and divide.

Grandma's kitchen had a mixed aura of strictness, care, fun and frolic,

We always remember grandma's kitchen for all the vibes and the comics.

- *Subholaxmi Ganguly.*

A Memory Where Time Stood Still

The morning sun would gently rise,
And light her kitchen's cozy guise.
With saree tucked and hair in bun,
She'd hum a tune, her day begun.

The shelves were lined with jars and tins,
Of pickled mangoes and crispy cookie bins.
Papads drying on the sill,
While tea brewed strong, and time stood still.

The cooking flame would softly glow,
By wooden pots lined row by row.
Brass vessels gleamed with seasoned grace,
Each held a world, a time, a place.

The scent of spices filled the air,

Of cumin, clove, and tender care.
Her hands, so worn yet full of might,
Turned simple meals to pure delight.

We'd gather round the wooden table,
She'd serve with joy, strong and stable.
No feast too grand, no dish too small,
Her cooking made it special all.

Stories flowed with every bite,
Of village days and lantern light.
Her voice, a thread of woven lore,
That made us beg to hear one more.

When thunder rolled and skies turned grey,
She'd fry up bhajis without delay.
The scent of rain and sizzling spice,
Made stormy days feel soft and nice.

Though years have passed, her voice is still,

In every spice and windowsill.

Her kitchen lives inside my heart,

A timeless, tender, treasured part.

- *Blessy Rani Jenefer S.*

Flavors of Grandma's Love

In Grandma's kitchen, mornings start,
With love she pours straight from her heart.
The kettle whistles, the butter melts,
Her gentle care is always felt.

The table waits with cups in line,
She fills each plate and says, "Now dine."
Her hands move slow, yet sure and kind,
With every stir, peace comes to mind.

The smell of curry, bread so warm,
A shelter safe from any storm.
Jars of pickles, sweets in a jar,
Remind me how her hugs still are.

Her apron stained with time and care,
Tells the stories resting there.

Of children grown, of songs once sung,
Of battles fought, of bells once rung.

The clock ticks soft, the sunlight glows,
Her wrinkled face in kindness shows.
And even when the room feels still,
Her kitchen hums with love until—

The world outside can fade away,
But in her kitchen, I can stay.
For every dish, each spoon, each pan,
Holds the magic of Grandma's hand.

- *Priyadharshini K.*

Grandma's Kitchen: Where Spices Whisper Stories

The wooden door creaks, the moment I nearby,
A world of comfort draws me here.
The smoky lamp, the warm clay floor,
A universe lives behind that door.

The fragrance of cardamom fills the air,
Turmeric glows with saffron's flair.
Coriander sings with pepper's bite,
Each spice a memory, burning bright.

The pickle jars shine in the morning sun,
A rainbow of patience, slowly spun.
Mango, lemon, chili red—
Each taste a tale of love she spread.

Her wrinkled hands, so steady, wise,

Fold the dough as stories rise.
The rolling pin hums its gentle song,
Teaching me roots where I belong.

The kettle hums like a temple bell,
Its echo carries what words can't tell.
Tea leaves swirl in the bubbling stream,
Pouring warmth into every dream.

She stirs the curry, her eyes aglow,
Adding more love than recipes show.
A pinch of salt, a smile, a prayer,
And magic fills the humble air.

No palace feast, no banquet grand,
Could match the grace of her gentle hand.
For in her kitchen, I understand—
Food is love, and love is land.

- *Dr. Richa Biswal.*

Grandma's Kitchen

The time passed quickly, but that kitchen prevails,
The scent of spicy spices, and the memory sustains,
Modern stoves took the place of ancient flames,
But the warmth of her cooking always remains.

Each roti she made was filled with love and care,
Her kitchen taught us the value of fair and share,
The pickle she made is now a treasure so rare,
The kitchen tells her story, steeped in many layers.

Grandma's kitchen was more than just a space,
It was childhood's warmth, her gentle embrace,
A forever memory in this busy race,
Our haven of love, our special place.

- *Sakshi Kshipra Singh.*

Grandma's Kitchens

A Beautiful lady, A Beautiful lady
"Hey what are you searching?"
A voice from back, sweet voice
"Searching chocolates grandma "
Grandma's Kitchens, Grandma's Kitchens
Every food item is found

Pickles, Pickles made from her
Kitchens is useless without her
Watching a Kitchens, Remembers
How she prepares food for us
Making buttermilk from her hand
Different taste, healthy food
She would love to prepares food
Her sweet voice, her love, her smiles
Missing a lot, Missing a lot
Can we bring the days back

Oh grandma, Oh grandma

Love & miss you a lot

Kitchens had created memories with grandma.

- *Divya D Nayak.*

Spices of Love in Grandma's Kitchen

In Grandma's kitchen, dawn begins,
With temple bells and gentle hymns.
The incense swirls, the ghee lamps glow,
And childhood memories softly flow.

The iron tawa hisses loud,
As rotis puff like clouds unbowed.
She hums a bhajan, voice so sweet,
While mustard seeds in oil compete.

Curry leaves crackle, their fragrance sings,
Turmeric shines like golden rings.
A pinch of hing, a drop of lime,
Transforms the taste with magic rhyme.

Pickle jars in the sunlight gleam,
Red with chili, green with dream.

Mango, lemon, or fiery tamarind,
Each jar a tale the years have pinned.

The brass lota filled with water pure,
A touch of tulsi, blessings sure.
The grinding stone, with rhythmic beat,
Echoes of patience, calm, complete.

In summer's heat, the aamras flows,
In winter's chill, til laddoo glows.
Monsoon nights with pakoras fried,
Chai in steel tumblers by her side.

Her recipes aren't written down,
They live in memory, time-worn, brown.
A fistful here, a dash of spice,
She cooks with heart, not with device.

Festival days, her kitchen shines,

With modaks, pedas, gujiyas fine.
The rangoli waits, the vessels gleam,
Her hands fulfill each festive dream.

Oh, Grandma's kitchen, India's heart,
A temple where love plays its part.
Not just for hunger, but for soul,
Her cooking makes the broken whole.

Each dish a blessing, warm, divine,
A sacred bond through food and time.
For in that hearth, I've always known,
The sweetest taste of home, my own.

- *Dr. Rutam Biswal.*

Theme: Home planet.

Writers:

- Malin Jenifer Raja.
- Divya D Nayak.
- Dr. Richa Biswal.
- Subholaxmi Ganguly.
- Blessy Rani Jenefer S.

Searching for my sweet comfort

Under the same sky,
Couldn't feel home.
Searching here and there,
Everywhere I roam.
Wandering with memories,
Where the stars above.
Roaming with dreams,
Looking the planet that I love.
Longing for earth,
The home's sweet comfort.
Feeling my planet's warmth,
In every endless night.
Love touches the sky,
With the moon's glow.
Missing my familiar place,
Where my memories grow.

Could hear the gentle lullaby,

In the void's silence.

Seeking the path,

Where I find my comfort space.

- *Malin Jenifer R.*

Home Planet

Greenery plants, Greenery plants

Yes, it's me Earth

Some take care of me and some destroy them

Everyone loves me,

Beautiful creatures I am.

Please don't destroy me

Stop Cutting Trees, Plant Trees

Keep clean and tidy

Home Planet, Home Planet

Save resources, Planted Trees.

\- *Divya D Nayak.*

Whispers of My Distant Sky

I walk among streets heavy with stone and smoke,
Where towers scrape the clouds,
And people rush like restless rivers,
Never pausing to breathe the silence of stars.
They see me as one of their own,
Yet my bones carry the memory of a different gravity,
My veins hum with the echo of a sky
Painted in colors Earth has never dreamed.
I remember my planet -
Where the oceans glowed with silver light,
And trees bent not with weight,
But with the joy of their own songs.
Where the night was not a curtain of darkness,
But a vast canvas brushed with starlight so close
You could cup them in your palms.
Here, on Earth, the sun burns too harsh,
The moon feels too lonely.

I search in rivers for the reflection of my skies,

But the water here is always hurried,

Always broken by stones.

How do I tell them -

These humans, so proud of their world -

That I am not at home?

That each breath I take tastes foreign,

That even the wind carries a language

I cannot quite understand?

On my planet, silence was never empty.

It was filled with the hum of constellations,

The low lullaby of twin suns dipping into the horizon,

The soft pulse of the earth beneath my feet

Like a mother whispering to her child.

Here, silence feels like exile.

A reminder that distance is not measured in miles,

But in the ache of belonging.

Yet sometimes, in the stillest hours of night,

When humans sleep and cities hush,

I look up -

And for a fleeting breath,

The stars remember me.

They lean closer,

As if trying to speak across the endless dark,

As if telling me:

"You are not lost,

You are a bridge between worlds."

And I wonder -

Perhaps Earth is not my prison,

But my pilgrimage.

Perhaps the longing I feel

Is not a curse,

But the thread tying two skies together.

Still, I dream -

Of the gentle weightlessness of my home planet,

Of the laughter of rivers that never rush,

Of a sky where my heart

Is not a stranger.

Until I return,

I will carry both worlds in me -

This Earth with its chaos and charm,

And my faraway planet with its eternal calm.

Two homes,

One soul.

Forever wandering between shadows and starlight.

\- *Dr. Richa Biswal.*

Longing For My Homeland

Came on a tour to the only place where life exists,

Stood in disbelief as from all sides heavy smoke and pollutants hissed.

Got stuck on this planet Earth due to an unforeseen situation,

Longed to go to my Home Planet - my safe place, my own station.

This Earth always pulls me towards itself, as if sticking me on the ground,

My eardrums seem to burst when it gets pierced by the intensified sound.

I want to go back to my planet where serenity and silence prevail,

I wish to see again how twin stars and constellations set sail.

Earth has green things called trees which seems cool,

But I see Earthlings cutting them recklessly - just like a fool.

I wish to show them what happens back at my home,

How we love our resources and keep them wrapped in a sheath of foam.

These days on Earth will be eternally remembered by me,

Not as cherished narratives but as lessons on how dutiful we should truly be,

Now, I wish to fly back to my zone as fast as I can,

Leaving behind my stories etched in the memories of Earth's people called man.

\- *Subholaxmi Ganguly.*

I Left My Sky Behind

I came from a world where the forests breathe,
Where voices bloom in crowded light.
Now Earth holds me in hush and stone,
Too still, too clean, too strangely right.

My planet sang in tangled vines,
In laughter loud and skies of moss.
Here silence wears a polished face,
And every joy feels like a loss.

I miss the crush of living sound,
The scent of soil, the pulse of rain.
This world is wide but not alive,
Its beauty dressed in quiet pain.

I speak to trees in broken tongue,
And dream of streets that danced with green.

Your gardens nod but do not know,
The wildness of the world I've seen.

Each night I trace the stars for signs,
A path that bends through time and dust.
I send my longing into space,
A prayer wrapped in ancient trust.

Return me to the noise and leaf,
To roots that held me like a song.
For even here, in exile's breath,
My heart still knows where I belong.

I wear my past like second skin,
Its colors faded, soft, and true.
Though time may stretch the space between,
It cannot dim the world I knew.

So let this Earth remain unknown,

A canvas I may never claim.

Still, in my chest, a forest grows,

And every leaf recalls its name.

\- *Blessy Rani Jenefer S.*

Theme: Goodbyes.

Writers:

- Malin Jenifer Raja.
- Divya D Nayak.
- Subholaxmi Ganguly.
- Blessy Rani Jenefer S.
- Dr. Rutam Biswal.
- Ananya Nayak.
- Priyadharshini K.
- Dr. Richa Biswal.

Friends' goodbye

School symphony, intertwined with emotions,
Memories created with laughter and tears.
Strangers became friends, where knowledge flows,
Laughter echoed where every memory glows.
School days cherished where dreams take flight,
Farewell whispers, new beginning await.
Tears dried with care, in learning corridors,
We've laughed & grown, in classrooms & courtyards.
School's farewell goodbye, our hearts remain tied,
The future beckons, our bond will never subside.
Farewell whispers a journey and a bond Devine,
Illuminating paths, our strong bonds remain.

- *Malin Jenifer R.*

Goodbye

Remember the time,

Happy & sweets moments

Last Goodbye, Last Goodbye

Can't expect this day

Where I will lose you

Missing the old memories

Silent tears, Silent tears

My Heart missing you

Can we meet in next lifetime

Always connected by love

Silly jokes, Silly laughs

Can we pause the world.

- *Divya D Nayak.*

Farewell Vibes

Gradually time flies, days pass, but memories stay,

Finally, the moment comes to bid a sweet goodbye on
the final day.

"Goodbye" signifies not the end but ' meet you soon',

This word recalls all the blissful mornings and nights of
full moon.

Teary eyes aren't meant for the goodbye biding times,

Nostalgic poems and sweet talks are the treasures which
actually then rhymes.

Whether I bid a goodbye or you do, the promise of
returning very soon is what really matters,

If goodbyes do turn into 'welcome back' on time, then
our heart really shatters.

- *Subholaxmi Ganguly.*

No Real Goodbye

When I said goodbye to you, my friend,
It wasn't just a simple end.
It felt like pages torn apart,
A quiet ache inside my heart.

I smiled, but it was bittersweet,
Like sunshine fading in retreat.
The laughter paused, the words ran dry,
And all I could do was sigh.

I felt the weight of all we shared,
The times you showed me that you cared.
The silly jokes, the late-night calls,
The way you caught me when I'd fall.

I didn't cry, not then, not loud,
But grief still wrapped me like a shroud.

A part of me walked off with you,
To chase the dreams, you're heading to.

Yet even as we said goodbye,
I knew this bond would never die.
For friends like you don't fade away,
You live in hearts where memories stay.

Though time may pass and seasons shift,
Your memory remains a gift.
In every step, in every sigh,
You're with me still - no real goodbye.

\- *Blessy Rani Jenefer S.*

Chapters of Farewell

A book lay open upon my knees,
Its pages stirred by a gentle breeze,
The words were glowing, soft and bright,
A lantern flame in the arms of night.
I read of laughter, hope, and skies,
Of golden dawns where dreams arise,
Yet as the lines began to fade,
I felt the sting of goodbyes made.

For every story holds a door,
A chapter closed, a "nevermore,"
And though the ink may still remain,
The heart relives the tender pain.
I've parted ways with papered friends,
With fates that met their sudden ends,
A knight who fell, a queen who wept,
A poet's vow the silence kept.

And just like books, so too is life,
A woven quilt of joy and strife,
Each meeting blooms, each parting burns,
The wheel of time forever turns.
When I said goodbye to you that day,
It felt like words had slipped away,
As if a story, torn in two,
Had lost its ending, lost its view.

Your voice, once inked upon my mind,
Now lingers faint, a ghost confined,
A dog-eared page I cannot find,
A farewell whispered to the wind.
Goodbyes are bookmarks left behind,
They mark the ache within the mind,
The places where the soul once dwelled,
The truths too heavy to be spelled.

Yet even endings shape our song,
They teach the heart where it belongs,
For every book that bids adieu,
Another waits, with skies bluer.
I learned from books what life made clear:
That love may leave, yet still stay nearby,
That chapter's end, yet never die,
They live in echoes, in the sky.

So, when the time to part is near,
I'll write our story crystal clear,
With ink of sorrow, quills of rain,
And bind it fast with threads of pain.
But know, though pages close today,
Our tale will never fade away,
For books and hearts are much the same -
Goodbyes may end, but not the flame.

- *Dr. Rutam Biswal.*

Goodbye

Goodbye, it's time to part,
Memories of yours will stay in my heart forever.
Though we are not near, you will always be near,
In my thoughts and in my memories my dear.

Wishing you well on your way,
May life bring joy, come what may.
Goodbye dear, don't forget,
You will always be loved and you will never regret.

- *Ananya Nayak.*

Beyond goodbyes

We laughed like rivers side by side,
Two souls in flow, one gentle tide.
But destiny, like a sudden storm,
Redrew the map, reshaped the norm.

Goodbyes were spoken, soft yet sore,
Like closing gently, a precious door.
Your voice still lingers, calm and near,
Like music my heart will always hear.

You are the moon to my darkest night,
A steady glow, a guiding light.
Though miles now stretch, both wide and long,
Our bond beats steady, fierce and strong.

Like roots of trees that hide below,
Our love runs deep; it will always grow.

Distance may scatter days apart,
But never the ties that bind our heart.

I see you in stars when skies are clear,
Each shining spark says you are near.
And when the wind begins to rise,
It carries whispers of your goodbyes.

So let the miles be vast, unkind,
They cannot sever what they can't find.
For brother and sister, heart to heart,
Are bound in ways no space can part.

And one sweet day, the roads will bend,
And bring me back to you, my friend.
Until that time, love lights the way -
Beyond goodbyes, we'll meet one day.

- *Priyadharshini K.*

When Goodbyes Burn Slow

Goodbyes are not thunder,
they do not crash all at once -
they linger,
like the echo of footsteps in a hallway,
like smoke that curls in the air
long after the flame has died.

I have tasted them on trembling lips,
a half-smile breaking into silence,
the weight of words unsaid
heavier than any suitcase carried away.

Sometimes, it is a whisper at the station,
the train swallowing distance faster
than the heart can measure.
Sometimes, it is in hospital corridors,
where the last look, the last breath,

becomes a permanent exile.
And sometimes—
it is not even spoken aloud.
It is felt in the spaces between texts,
in the phone that doesn't ring anymore,
in the empty chair across the table
that pretends it is still occupied.

I have said goodbye with my hands shaking,
with my eyes refusing to betray
the storm inside me.
And I have received goodbyes
that left me hollow,
as though someone carved out the walls of my chest
and filled it with silence.

But perhaps—
every goodbye is also a teacher.
It reminds us that love is mortal in form,

eternal in memory.
That the heart breaks, yes,
but it also remembers,
it grows,
it learns the art of carrying absence
as if it were another kind of presence.

So here's to the goodbyes—
to the ones we say,
to the ones we hear,
to the ones we never got to whisper.
Each one is a scar,
but also a song—
a soft hymn that teaches us
how to keep walking,
even when our shadows
walk alone.

- *Dr. Richa Biswal.*

Theme: Uncertainty.

Writers:

- Malin Jenifer Raja.
- Dr. Richa Biswal.
- Divya D Nayak.
- Dr. Rutam Biswal.
- Ananya Nayak.
- Subholaxmi Ganguly.
- Blessy Rani Jenefer S.
- Shruti Samskruti.
- Sakshi Kshipra Singh.

The whispering voices.

Choices swirled around me, which one is to pursue,
Each seemed right, my heart felt blue.
Fear of wrong choice, I wandered alone,
Each choice a possibility, yet none seemed mu=y own.
I stood still, the scales of doubt,
Each door a potential, yet neither felt right.
I searched for clarity, in the dark of night,
Torn between two choices, a difficult fight.
With paths unclear, I stood so still,
Waves of doubt crash, my heart is unfulfilled.
Not knowing which path, I'm lost & alone,
My heart & mind disagree; it presses me down.
The weight of uncertainty, my heart is turned to stone,
Time ticked on, I yearn for a beacon.

- *Malin Jenifer R.*

Between Two Roads

I stood before the crossroads,
heart heavy, hands trembling,
each path whispering its own promise,
each silence louder than the other.

The left road carried comfort—
a meadow I had known before,
safe as a mother's lap,
but shadowed by the weight of "what if."

The right road gleamed with mystery,
its horizon wrapped in fog,
a thrill that tasted of freedom,
yet the fear of falling clung to me.

I turned my gaze inward,
but even my heart was divided—

half yearning for shelter,

half aching to fly.

Uncertainty sat beside me,

like an old friend I never invited,

reminding me of every doubt,

every wound I hadn't healed.

And so I lingered there,

between choices, between breaths,

learning that sometimes -

even in indecision -

life teaches us who we are becoming.

- *Dr. Richa Biswal.*

Uncertainty

A Time we spent

With family, with friends

It's uncertain, It's uncertain

Be good with everyone

Can't say they are with us tomorrow

Time is uncertainty

Respect each other

Create memories

That's life.

- *Divya D Nayak.*

Between the Pages of Doubt

I sat before my desk one night,
My lamp the only source of light.
Books in a tower, papers wide,
Yet still the answers seemed to hide.

Should I prepare for what is safe,
A steady path, a sheltered waif?
Or chase a course where passion sings,
Though filled with unknown wanderings?

Mathematics whispered, Stay with me,
History murmured, Set thought free.
Science demanded endless hours,
While literature bloomed with gentle powers.

I flipped through notes, my mind a storm,
Each formula refused to form.

One moment I was sure, then not,
A prisoner of my tangled thought.

The clock struck twelve, my pen stood still,
My heart bent under restless will.
For every subject pulled apart
The fragile focus of my heart.

I asked myself, Which dream is mine?
To draw in labs, or write in line?
To serve in halls of learned pride,
Or let my art be not denied?

The pages blurred with sleepless eyes,
The future loomed, a masked disguise.
And in that moment, I could see—
Uncertainty's true test of me.

But as I wrote my fears away,

The ink gave shape to break of day.
For though I waver, stumble, fall,
The act of writing clears it all.

Studies may daunt, the choices vast,
Exams may judge, but doubts don't last.
For every question, wrong or right,
Becomes a poem in the night.

So if you find yourself unsure,
Your dreams divided, none secure -
Take up the pen, let thoughts be freed,
For clarity grows when words take seed.

- *Dr. Rutam Biswal.*

Uncertainty

Time, we spent with each other,

It's uncertain, let's be good with All,

Let's respect each other,

Let's be Smarter,

Time is Uncertainty,

Let's Create Memories,

Because Memories is a Treasure that we feel happy by seeing it,

Life is uncertain that we don't know what's the next,

But we will face it with courage and respect.

So Let's Respect Each other and Let's Create Memories

Thats Life.

- *Ananya Nayak.*

Between The River And It's Banks

Variety of opportunities waved at me,
To correctly choose was the master key.
Uncertain I was - staring at the future,
Had to choose between an anthology or an aperture.
Streams, subjects, practical - each had something special,
Puzzled I was on which one to nestle.

Career and passion both were very dear,
Which one to embrace and adopt, I wasn't clear.
Light shined on all my ways, yet I felt dim,
Closed my eyes and started murmuring God's hymn.
The more roads, the more ways, the more it was fun,
But at the end, a single destination had to be the ultimate one.

Uncertainty in life is the biggest blockage in head,
The real remedy then is our parents' wisdom's shade.
What is right and what is wrong is the hardest thing to decide,

At this crucial juncture, God's temple is the safest place to reside.

- *Subholaxmi Ganguly.*

The Crossroads of Choice

Two roads stretched out before my feet,
Both paved with dreams, both incomplete.
One whispered books and lecture halls,
The other echoed office calls.
A cap and gown in distant light,
Promised wisdom, future bright.
But pay checks glimmered in my hand,
A chance to rise, to take a stand.

I weighed the hours, the sleepless nights,
The thesis born in coffee fights.
Against the grind of nine-to-five,
Where purpose and pay check might collide.
My parents spoke of stable ground,
My mentors urged me to rebound.
I scribbled plans, erased them twice,
Each option came with its own price.

Would I regret the path not taken?
Would either leave my soul forsaken?
I feared the silence of the wrong,
The echo of a choice too long.
But in that storm of doubt and dread,
I found a voice inside my head:
"You're not defined by one decision -
Your life's a canvas, not a prison."

So, I choose - not perfect, not precise,
But with a heart that rolled the dice.
And whether books or boardroom walls,
I'd learn to rise through every fall.
Now I walk where both paths blend,
A scholar's mind, a worker's end.
In books I grow, in work I strive,
Two dreams, one life, both kept alive.

- *Blessy Rani Jenefer.S.*

The Hour of Maybe

I stood at the crosswalk of a half-lit day, day.

Two tickets in my pocket, neither one to stay, day.

One road hummed with promise, a bright busy road, road.

The other whispered comfort, a slow-moving road, road.

My watch beat a question, each tick stealing time, time.

My mouth rehearsed courage, my hands could not mime, time.

I pictured the future behind every closed door, door.

Each key felt convincing and then felt like more, door.

My heart sent invitations I could not impart, heart.

It folded its maps and folded my heart, heart.

Friends drew sharp arrows; my doubt drew a home, home.

I wanted to follow, but I wanted to roam, home.

The sky offered mercy, a cloud soft and clear, clear.

I breathed in the not-knowing and kept it near, clear.

At last, I let maybe be my quiet, shy guide, guide.

And for once I lived well inside not to decide, decide.

- *Shruti Samskruti.*

Between Dusk and Dawn

I'm standing alone in a vast, murky lawn,
Torn between the beauty of dusk and dawn,
The sunset feels like the end, so as sunrise,
But how do I know which decision is wise?!
The sun lights the path for a warm new day,
But so does the moon in the dark far away,
Two jewels of nature, both different, and divine,
But how do I know which path is mine?!

The two roads ahead look like fire and ice,
One screams freedom, and the other of ties,
I watch for the sky to find the right sign,
Which is the quest where my stars align?
Maybe there is no answer, wrong or right,
I've to welcome both the dark and the light,
The journey of life is uncertain on each stride,
So, I walk through the lawn with hope by my side.

\- *Sakshi Kshipra Singh.*

Theme: Misfits.

Writers:

- Malin Jenifer Raja.
- Subholaxmi Ganguly.
- Dr. Rutam Biswal.
- Tr Mrs Sunita Martins.
- Divya D Nayak.
- Dr. Richa Biswal.
- Blessy Rani Jenefer S.
- Sakshi Kshipra Singh.

The weight of loneliness

I'm lost in the sea, where I don't find my song,
I'm surrounded by people, but don't belong.
Like a puzzle piece, can't find a way,
I'm stuck on the bank, with nothing to say.
I wear a mask, I'm invisible too,
Longing for roots, that's real and new.
The world keeps spinning, like a river's stream,
I'm a stranger here, with a silent dream.
Longing for a touch, like a leaf on wind,
I try to fit in, but feeling drained.
I'm swept away in a bond that's made,
A solitary soul among the crowd.

- *Malin Jenifer R.*

Misfits

A Coal Piece in a Gold Chain

With water molecules all around, I feel like oil.

Talking to them makes me perceive that I'm on an alien soil.

Sitting amidst a group but can't engage in talks,

The reason being the discussed topics aren't of my sorts.

Minor conversations if at all, sometimes abruptly stops,

Lift my eyes and surprisingly see that some faces sadly drop.

My soul hints that I'm a misfit in this group,

Gradually, I retreat back mentally out of this loop.

\- *Subholaxmi Ganguly.*

The Lantern Outside the Crowd

I stand apart where voices blend,
A quiet soul that can't pretend.
Their circles spin, their echoes cheer,
Yet something tells me I'm not nearby.

They weave their tales like threads of flame,
But none are stitched with my own name.
I try to join, my words feel small,
They rise like smoke, then fade and fall.

A river flows, I drift as sand,
The current pulls, I miss the land.
Their boats are full, they sail with ease,
While I am stranded by the seas.

They shine like suns in skies so wide,
While I remain the moon that hides.

Their rhythm beats in practiced time,
Yet mine's a different, ragged rhyme.

I'm not a jewel in velvet light,
But just a stone in endless night.
Still stones can whisper, stones can sing,
Of mountain roots and secret spring.

So though I walk a separate lane,
And bear the weight of quiet pain,
I'll guard my spark, I'll keep it true,
For misfit hearts burn brighter too.

When all the stars look just the same,
A lone one carves its untold flame.
And though I wander, out of place,
I hold my sky, my sacred space.

- *Dr. Rutam Biswal.*

Misfits

There is no one in this world who is but actually a Misfit

It must probably have been the circumstances that lead to one becoming a Misfit.

What is this life if we do not accept others in our lives

with open arms and open hearts and make them feel at ease and not as Misfit.

Let's bring about a change in the life of those who are less fortunate

and who are waiting to meet people and are no longer Misfit.

Everyone is unique and have different thought processes,

It to understand and accept others the way they are even if they are Misfits.

Being a Misfit is not a flaw but a potential advantage to bring about

innovation and prosperity in their own lives and we still call them Misfits.

Let us all embrace all the Misfits and let us all make them feel that

they are the best creation of the almighty though some of us still call them Misfits

- *Tr Mrs Sunita Martins.*

Misfits

Someone, Someone
Not acceptable, not acceptable
Change in behaviour, Change in attitude
Some Dancers who are hated
Due to incoordination and bad attitude
Everyone is different and unique
Someone at party is unknown to other
Creates misfits between both of them
Someone is personally misfits
Due to half-hearted personality
They love to be respected by others
Treated kindly and equal but separately
Someone who do not follow social norms
They are expected as misfits.

\- *Divya D Nayak.*

The Song of Misfits

We sit at the edge of crowded rooms,
our laughter stitched with silent looms,
while others weave their tapestries bright,
we hold our threads in shadowed light.

The circle forms, their voices blend,
a chorus we cannot comprehend.
Their rhythms pulse, their gestures glide—
yet something keeps us just outside.

We are the mismatched notes in a song,
the lines that wander, the brushstrokes wrong,
the puzzle pieces carved too rare
to fit the patterns waiting there.

Our shoes don't march to their parade,
our hearts refuse the games they've played.

We dream in colours they cannot name,
and carry fires they cannot tame.

Oh, how they laugh with easy grace,
while we search mirrors for a face—
a self that speaks, a voice that rings,
a pair of unnoticed, folded wings.

But maybe misfits are not mistakes,
nor broken glass that silence breaks.
Perhaps we are the quiet streams
that carve new mountains out of dreams.

Perhaps we are the whispered stars
that linger long when night is sparse.
Perhaps we are the roots below,
the hidden strength that helps things grow.

So let them gather, hand in hand,

upon their well-worn, trusted land.
We'll walk the wild, uncertain skies,
and write our truth where freedom lies.

For misfits are the sparks of change,
the ones who dare, the ones who range.
Not meant to blend, but meant to blaze,
to scatter light in endless ways.

So here we stand, outside their wall,
alone, yet not forsaken at all.
For every misfit, torn apart,
still holds the cosmos in their heart.

- *Dr. Richa Biswal.*

The Quiet Edge

I stand among the laughing crowd,
Their voices rise - a woven shroud.
Yet every thread, though bright and bold,
Slips past my fingers, leaves me cold.

Their stories bloom like springtime air,
But none take root within my care.
I smile, I nod, I play the part,
While silence gardens in my heart.

A stranger in familiar skin,
I knock, but never quite get in.
Their rhythm pulses, smooth and clear,
A song I cannot seem to hear.

I'm not the echo they expect,
My thoughts diverge; my truths deflect.

They speak in codes I cannot crack,
And every step, I'm holding back.

It's not disdain, nor bitter pride,
Just longing I can't seem to hide.
To be a note within their chord,
Not just a shadow they ignored.

Yet in this space, I learn to see,
The quiet strength of being me.
Though I don't fit their perfect frame,
I still exist - I still remain.

\- *Blessy Rani Jenefer.S.*

Out of the Rhyme

I look around at the smiles in the crowd,
The whispers of them seem so loud,
I smile with them side by side,
But I know that's a mask I can't hide.

Their words don't ever feel like mine,
The dreams they share, don't match my twine,
I hum the songs they sing all the time,
Even though I know I'm out of the rhyme.

I stand with them, but alone in my heart,
I'm the misfit, near-yet so apart,
But I have a world where I sing the song I like,
And paint my skies with colors I strike.

- *Sakshi Kshipra Singh.*

The Misfit I am

I am the echo that doesn't return the same,
a rhythm off-beat, a fire untamed.
The world hands me boxes, neat and square,
but I slip through the cracks - I don't belong there.

I am the wild note in a practiced song,
the question mark where answers belong.
They see crooked edges, I see hidden art,
a map of galaxies stitched on my heart.

In a crowd of mirrors, I stand un-reflected,
their polished smiles leave me unaffected.
I wear my silence like second skin,
yet storms brew fiercely deep within.

I am the shadow they can't pin down,
the wanderer, neither lost nor found.

They call me different - I wear it proud,

my voice may be quiet, but it sings loud.

I am the misfit, a spark in disguise,

a constellation beyond their skies.

Unfitting, unbroken, wholly my own,

I am the seed that grows where nothing is sown.

\- *Priyadharshini K.*

www.ingramcontent.com/pod-product-compliance
Lightning Source LLC
Chambersburg PA
CBHW062111160726
48282CB00026B/753
* 9 7 8 8 1 9 9 1 3 5 7 4 1 *